THE WILD WATER MYSTERY AT Niagara Falls

First Edition ©2009 Carole Marsh/Gallopade International/Peachtree City, GA
Current Edition ©June 2014
Ebook edition ©2011
All rights reserved.
Manufactured in Peachtree City, GA

Carole Marsh Mysteries™ and its skull colophon are the property of Carole Marsh and Gallopade International.

Published by Gallopade International/Carole Marsh Books. Printed in the United States of America.

Managing Editor: Sherry Moss
Senior Editor: Janice Baker
Assistant Editor: Susan Walworth
Cover Design: Yvonne Ford
Cover Photo Credits: shutterstock.com
Picture Credits: Lori J. White
Content Design and Illustrations: Yvonne Ford

Gallopade International is introducing SAT words that kids need to know in each new book that we publish. The SAT words are bold in the story. Look for this special logo beside each word in the glossary. Happy Learning!

LEGO® is a trademark of the LEGO Group.

Gallopade is proud to be a member and supporter of these educational organizations and associations:

American Booksellers Association
American Library Association
International Reading Association
National Association for Gifted Children
The National School Supply and Equipment Association
The National Council for the Social Studies
Museum Store Association
Association of Partners for Public Lands
Association of Booksellers for Children
Association for the Study of African American Life and History
National Alliance of Black School Educators

Once upon a time...

Papa said …

Why don't you set the stories in real locations?

That's a great idea! And if I do that, I might as well choose real kids as characters in the stories! But which kids would I pick?

MIMI, PICK ME, PICK ME!

ME, TOO, MIMI, PICK ME, TOO!

Christina

Grant

Pick me!

You two really are characters, that's all I've got to say!

Yes you are! And, of course I choose you! But what should I write about?

 National parks!

SCARY PLACES!

FAMOUS PLACES!

FUN PLACES!

Disney World!

New York City!

Dracula's Castle

GRAND CANYON

On the *Mystery Girl* airplane ...

I CaN FLY US anyWHeRe!

Or aboard
the *Mimi!*

Take me to the
Forbidden City!

Or by surfboard,
rickshaw,
motorbike,
camel ...

All great ideas!
I can put a lot of history,

MYSTERY,

legend, lore, and **laughs** in
the books! We can use other boys and girls
in the books. It will be educational and fun!

Good
stuff!

9

Can I apply?

And so, Mimi, Papa, Christina, and Grant took off aboard the *Mystery Girl* and America's National Mystery Book Series—where the adventure is real and so are the characters! —was born.

START YOUR ADVENTURE TODAY!

READ THE BOOK!

GO ONLINE!

TRACK YOUR ADVENTURES!

APPLY TO BE A CHARACTER!

ABOUT THE CHARACTERS

Christina
Yother
Age 10

Grant
Yother
Age 7

David
Hemphill
Age 10

Allison
Cooper
Age 10

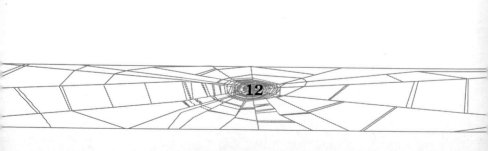

1
ROLL OUT THE BARREL

"Christina! Look out!" Grant yelled in panic as he watched a massive, wooden barrel rolling straight toward his sister.

But Christina could not hear her brother over the thundering sound of Niagara Falls. Mesmerized, she kept staring through the mist at the mighty rushing water.

Grant lunged for Christina, pushing her against a metal railing and out of the barrel's path. She was safe, but Grant was not. Wide eyed, he watched the barrel take aim at him.

Suddenly, a glint of silver flashed in the autumn sunlight. It was a wheelchair and the boy in it was rolling between Grant and the barrel! As the barrel's corner caught the boy's wheel, it popped into the air and jumped off the sidewalk. The wayward barrel raced over the damp grass, collided with a park bench, and began to wobble wildly.

Splintered wood flew everywhere and a shower of colorful fall leaves rained to the ground as the barrel crashed into a tree.

"Whew!" Grant grabbed his chest in relief as he looked over at his sister.

"Was that barrel headed for me?" Christina asked, confused.

Before Grant could answer, the boy in the wheelchair joined them.

"Are you OK?" he asked.

"I'm sure my ribs will be sore tomorrow," Christina answered, rubbing her side.

"If you hadn't rolled in front of that barrel, I'd be squashed flat as a pancake right now," Grant added.

"Yes, thank you," Christina said as she self-consciously combed her long brown hair with her fingers.

Spinning his wheelchair around, the boy said, "Let's take a look at it!"

As they headed toward the barrel's remains, Christina asked, "Did you see where it came from?"

"No," the boy answered. "That's what's so strange about it. When people visit Niagara Falls, they expect to see a barrel going over the falls, not rolling down the sidewalk."

Grant, who had run ahead, reached the barrel first. "Looks empty!" he shouted.

"Do you think someone was planning to use it to ride over the falls?" Christina asked the boy in the wheelchair.

"Doing any kind of stunt like that is illegal," he answered. "I don't think they'd try it in broad daylight."

"Look at this," Grant said when they joined him beside the barrel. "It looks like some kind of crest," he remarked, tracing the strange mark with his finger.

"One thing's for sure," Christina said, picking up one of the broken boards. "This barrel will never hold anything again."

As Christina turned the board over in her hands, she was surprised to see words written in charcoal.

"What does this mean?" she asked, showing the boys.

JOIN THE RANKS AND ROLL!

"It looks like that barrel did have something inside," Grant exclaimed. "A clue!"

"Grant, don't start..." Christina began to chastise her brother, but something else grabbed her attention. A redheaded man wearing a bright yellow raincoat darted from behind a nearby tree.

I wonder if he was watching us, Christina thought.

Her thoughts were interrupted when the boy in the wheelchair spoke. "I don't have a clue what the barrel business is all about, but I'm glad you're both OK. I have to be heading home."

"Wait," Christina said. "You saved my brother's life, and I don't even know your name."

"David Hemphill," the boy answered. "I hope you enjoy your visit to Canada!"

2

AWESOME AQUA

"What a strange **coincidence**!" Christina told Grant as they looked for their grandparents. "I wanted to learn about the daredevils who have tried to conquer Niagara Falls, but I didn't know I'd get that close to a barrel so soon!"

Not wanting to worry Mimi and Papa, the siblings agreed to keep the barrel story between them.

"It probably just fell off a truck," Christina reassured her brother, tousling his blonde curls that had become ringlets in the moist air near the falls.

Still, Christina realized that mystery always seemed to find them. And if they had already found one clue, more would certainly follow.

"I saw them first!" Christina shouted over the falls' constant roar as she dashed ahead of Grant toward their grandparents.

Christina was sure she had the best grandparents in the world. Mimi and Papa, as she and Grant affectionately called them, often included them on trips to interesting places all around the world.

When they planned an Amtrak trip from Atlanta, Georgia to the Niagara Falls region, Grant and Christina were ecstatic. It was their first trip to Canada and they were going to be among the 14 million people who visit the falls each year! And since they were on fall break from school, it was also perfect timing.

Mimi wrote children's mystery books, and sometimes did research for her stories while they traveled. But on this trip, Grant was doing the research. He had a history project on the War of 1812 due after fall break.

"I'll get an 'A' for sure!" he had boasted.

Breathless from her sprint, Christina reached her grandparents.

"You sure...are easy...to spot...in a crowd!" she gasped.

"Whatever do you mean?" Mimi asked, striking a pose in her red vinyl hat, sunshine-yellow jacket, faded jeans, and shiny red boots.

As Christina giggled, Mimi added, "These boots are waterproof. When your feet get wet exploring Niagara Falls, you may wish you had some!"

"I'll take my chances," Christina said, turning up her nose at Mimi's fashion sense.

Papa didn't stand out nearly as much in his cowboy hat, jeans, and chocolate-brown cowboy boots. "So, what do you kids think of Niagara Falls?" he asked.

"Well, it's big!" Grant answered.

"And wet!"

"Glad you noticed that, Grant," Papa said with a laugh.

"One more thing," Grant added. "It's shaped like a horseshoe!"

"That's right, Grant," Papa said. "Many people call the falls here on the Canadian side the Horseshoe Falls. The other set of falls you can see from here are the American Falls. They are on American soil."

"I could stare at the falls for hours!" Christina said. "The flowing water looks like sparkling liquid hair!"

"That's the dumbest thing I've ever heard!" Grant said. "The way the water spills over the rim sort of reminds me of the time the toilet overflowed in my bathroom!"

"And you thought what I said was dumb?" Christina asked, turning to look at her brother.

Grant was on a roll. "Yeah, and see all that steam down there at the bottom of the falls?" Grant asked. "That reminds me of when Mimi cooks spaghetti!"

"Oh, brother!" Christina said. "First of all, Grant, that's not steam, because the water isn't hot. That's mist!"

Papa decided it was time to interrupt the bickering. "You'll get to know the falls up close and personal tomorrow," he said with a wink.

"What do you mean?" Grant asked.

Mimi answered, "You know Papa always has an adventure up his sleeve. But now, the only adventure I want is to find our bed and breakfast."

"Our bed and breakfast?" Grant asked. "Don't we need to find a hotel first?"

Mimi laughed. "A bed and breakfast is a type of hotel," she explained. "It's just feels a lot more like home. And they serve breakfast!"

"I'm for that!" Grant exclaimed. "Hearing all this running water makes me have to go!"

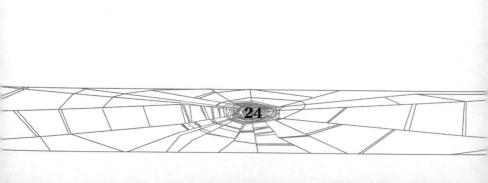

3
BED, BREAKFAST, AND BOOOOO!

"Are you sure this is it?" Grant asked warily, as Papa parked their baby blue rental car in front of the bed and breakfast.

"This is it!" Papa replied cheerfully.

"Looks like a Halloween house to me," Grant observed, eyeing the steep roof, turret, and the gingerbread trim around the porch.

"It's a Victorian mansion, Grant," Christina said.

"Yes," Mimi continued. "It reminds you of Halloween, because pictures you see of haunted houses are often Victorian-type houses. That doesn't mean that all Victorian houses are haunted, though."

"What exactly is a Victorian house?" Grant asked.

"Victorian houses were built between 1837 and 1901 during the reign of Queen Victoria, who was queen of England," Mimi explained.

"She was also queen of Canada, Mimi," Christina added. "Remember Great Britain and Canada share the same monarch."

"That's right!" Mimi said, excited at Christina's knowledge.

"Love the history lesson," Papa interrupted, "but let's get unpacked and continue it over dinner. I'm starving."

"We can't eat dinner here," Grant said. "It's a bed and BREAKFAST, not a bed and DINNER."

"Don't worry, Grant," Papa said. "We'll have dinner in the town of Niagara Falls."

"Welcome! Welcome!" A rather plump lady with a thick British accent greeted them at the door. "Allison and I have been expecting you!" she said. "I'm Ms. Bumpus, maid of this grand old lady, The Victoria. Sorry the mistress of the house couldn't be here to welcome you, but she's on a business trip in the States. This is her daughter, Allison Cooper. You're our only guests, so we're glad to have the company."

Christina thought it was odd that a housekeeper in the 21st century was dressed like Ms. Bumpus. She was wearing a long black dress covered in front by a white lace apron. Black pointed shoes peeked from under her skirt and red hair tumbled from under a frilly lace cap.

"I'll be happy to show you to your room," Ms. Bumpus said, grabbing Mimi's suitcase. "Allison, why don't you show the kids to their rooms?"

Grant and Christina followed Allison out of the foyer into an eerie, dark hallway. As they started up a curving staircase, each stair creaked on cue.

"Isn't it spooky to live here?" Grant asked Allison.

Allison flashed Grant a smile. She was a pretty girl with wavy, dark hair and brown eyes. "I've never lived anywhere else, so I'm used to it," she answered. "I'm used to The Victoria's sounds and moods."

When Grant realized his room was across the wide hall from Christina's room, he wished for once they were staying together. But he was relieved to see that his room had a television.

"Great!" he said. "I can play the video games I brought!"

"Enjoy your stay," Allison said, just like an innkeeper.

"Thanks, Allison," Christina replied. "Grant, I'll meet you in the hall after I wash up."

Grant began rummaging through his suitcase for his favorite video game until a strange noise stopped him. Sure it was his imagination, he started digging through his clothing again until he heard another sound. This time, he was sure he heard the muffled meow of a cat.

"Here kitty, kitty," Grant called. The sound grew louder, but Grant could tell it wasn't in the room with him.

"Must be coming from the room next door," he thought.

As Grant turned to walk back to his suitcase, however, his shirt sleeve caught on a piece of molding that framed a section of the wall beside the fireplace. Knowing what Mimi would say if he ripped one of his good shirts, he worked carefully to free the snag. But when he leaned against the wall for one last tug, the wall moved!

"This really is a haunted house!" he said to h i m s e l f .
Through the crack that had opened in the wall, Grant could see two eyes glowing. 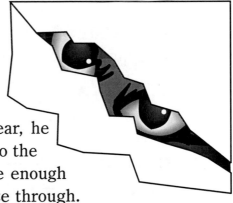 Quivering with fear, he pushed the wall so the opening was wide enough for him to squeeze through.

"SWOOSH!"

Something shot past Grant in the dim light. Stumbling forward, Grant caught his balance on something round and hard that rocked with his weight.

"Grant! Are you ready?" he heard his sister yell from the hallway.

Grant darted back through the wall's opening and ran to tell his sister what he had seen. "Christina, you're n-n-not going to b-b-believe this!" he stuttered.

"I f–f–found a s–s–secret room with b–barrels in it! And I think a c–c–cat was in there too!"

"Are you serious?" Christina said in disbelief.

"Come in here, I'll show you," Grant replied, grabbing her arm.

But when Grant took Christina to the spot where the wall had parted, it was closed tight. No amount of pushing or pulling could open it.

Looking at her brother in disgust, Christina scolded him. "Stop trying to scare me, Grant!"

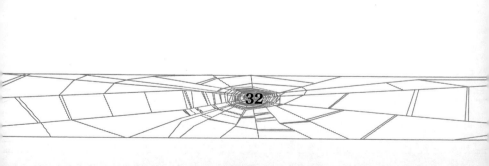

4

MAID OF THE MIST

"Why is Canadian bacon round?" Grant asked as he wolfed down a breakfast of waffles, eggs, and three slices of Canadian bacon.

"Never thought of that," Ms. Bumpus replied. "Why is American bacon in strips?"

"Because that's the shape bacon's supposed to be!" Grant answered quickly.

As Allison giggled at Grant, Christina asked her, "Do you have a cat?"

"No," Allison said. "But Mr. Mudgers visits us often."

Before Allison could explain, the doorbell interrupted the conversation.

"I'll get it!" Allison cried, jumping out of her chair.

When Allison returned, the kids were surprised to see David Hemphill with her.

She introduced him to Mimi and Papa, but as she started to introduce Christina and Grant, David stopped her.

"We met yesterday," he said with a mischievous grin.

"Yes," Christina said, returning the smile. "We met at the falls."

"We're going for a ride on the *Maid of the Mist*," Mimi said, looking at Allison and David. "Would you like to come along with us? We'd love to have some native tour guides."

"Sure," David said. "My Uncle Bob is captain of the *Maid*, so maybe I can get him to take us extra close to the falls."

"I never pass up an opportunity to get misted on Niagara Falls' most famous boat!" Allison exclaimed.

"Would you like to come along, Ms. Bumpus?" Mimi asked.

"Oh no!" she replied. "I'm a landlubber myself!"

"The lines of people boarding *Maid of the Mist* get very long later in the day," David said. "We'd better hurry to the falls."

At the dock, the entire group looked like strange blue ghosts as they pulled on thin plastic rain ponchos for their voyage.

"Now I know how garbage feels," Grant said, pulling the sticky plastic away from his skin.

"Yeah, I feel like Little Blue Riding Hood," Christina added.

"You'll soon be glad you have that on," Allison warned. "This will be the wettest ride you've ever taken!"

"I'm prepared!" Mimi cried, showing off her waterproof red boots once more.

Papa struggled to pull the poncho hood over his cowboy hat. Finally giving up, he said, "I'm sure my hat is waterproof too."

"You should've left that hat in the car," Mimi said with a frown.

"Cowboys never leave their hats in the car," he replied.

As they boarded the boat, Christina noticed a young man mopping the deck. To her surprise, he had red hair and was wearing a yellow raincoat, just like the mysterious man she had seen the day before.

"Who's that?" Christina asked David.

"Must be a new deckhand," David answered. "I'll be back. I'm going to find my uncle."

"Welcome aboard *Maid of the Mist*," Captain Bob said when David returned with him. "I see that David has led you to the starboard side, so you can get as wet as possible!"

"Gee, thanks, David," Christina said with a frown.

"Will we cross the border to the American Falls too?" Grant asked.

"Sure will," the captain replied. "You know the border between our countries lies right in the middle of the Niagara River, so sometimes one side of the *Maid* is in the United States while the other side is in Canada! Enjoy your voyage!"

As the *Maid* chugged through the mist toward Horseshoe Falls, Christina just knew it was going to be even more awesome than seeing the falls from the top.

"I feel like we're going inside a thundercloud," she shouted over the constant roar of the falling water. "It's wet and LOUD!"

"I feel like I'm inside a toilet bowl and someone has flushed!" Grant screamed.

"Kids, look at the rainbow!" Mimi shrieked with delight as she aimed her waterproof disposable camera at the colorful sight. "We're going to sail right through it!"

What started as a gentle mist became a torrent of water droplets as the boat pulled close to the powerful cascade. Christina couldn't suppress her laugh as she watched her tall Papa struggling to keep dry as his blue poncho flapped wildly in the wind.

Christina pulled her plastic hood tight around her face, wiped the water from her eyes, and stared in awe at the gigantic sheet of water towering 170 feet above her.

"This makes me feel so small," she shouted at David who had pushed his chair beside her.

"This is what Niagara is all about," he nodded in agreement. "That's 600,000 gallons coming over the falls each second."

Suddenly, Christina saw something brown come over the crest of the falls and disappear in the white foam boiling on top of the Niagara River's green water. She wiped her eyes again.

She looked over at Grant, who was pointing wildly.

"Did you see it?" he yelled. "Did you see the barrel?"

Did you see it?

5
BARREL OF GHOSTS?

Grant peeled the soggy socks from his feet and stretched out his toes in the breeze.

"I brought plenty of Niagara Falls with me as a souvenir," he said.

"Yep," Papa teased. "You really 'soaked' it all in, didn't you?"

"Grant!" Mimi exclaimed. "Take those wet socks off that picnic basket right now! Our lunch is in there!"

Across the park, Allison spotted a gathering of people under a white tent. "Oh, look!" she exclaimed. "Someone is getting married. The bride looks so pretty!"

"Do many people come to Niagara Falls to get married?" Christina asked, as they basked in the noon-day sun at Kingsbridge Park and ate the ham and cheese sandwiches Ms. Bumpus had packed for them.

"Are you kidding?" Allison said. "After the falls, marriage is what Niagara is most famous for. Its nickname is the 'Honeymoon Capital of the World'."

"Speaking of couples, how did you and David meet?" Allison asked.

After she shared their barrel meeting experience, Christina continued, "I think we might have seen another barrel go over the falls today! I sure would like to learn more about daredevils and barrels at Niagara Falls."

"We should visit the IMAX Theater and the Niagara Falls Daredevil Gallery," Allison suggested.

Papa, who was several yards away sharing a bunch of grapes with Mimi, interrupted. "Do you kids feel like visiting the IMAX Theater before we return to The Victoria?"

"Papa, were you **eavesdropping**?" Christina asked.

"Now you know I'd never do such a thing, little missy!" Papa said in his best cowboy drawl.

"So, what are we waiting for?" Christina replied. "Let's go!"

At the IMAX Theater, the six story-tall movie screen and surround sound put them once again in the middle of Niagara Falls.

"This is almost like being back on the *Maid of the Mist*," Grant observed, peering at the water falling all around him.

"Yes, it is," Mimi agreed. "But much drier!"

The movie narrator told the geologic history of how the falls formed when glaciers retreated and how during the next 50,000 years, experts believe that erosion will slowly bring the down the height of the falls until they no longer exist.

Christina gripped the bar in front of her nervously as she watched the story of The Great Blondin, an acrobat who crossed the Niagara Gorge several times on a tightrope in 1859.

But most interesting to Christina was the story of Annie Taylor, a widowed schoolteacher. On her 63rd birthday in 1901, Annie and her kitten survived a trip over the falls in a barrel. She was quoted as saying, "No one ought ever do that again."

As soon as Christina strolled into the adjoining Niagara Falls Daredevil Gallery and saw the actual barrels and other contraptions people had used to go over the falls, she realized Annie's advice had not been taken.

"Wow, some of these don't look like barrels at all," Grant said as he explored the displays. The vessels Dave Munday took over the falls during the 1980s and 1990s captured Grant's imagination. One was silver metal contraption that looked like a spaceship. Another was completely round like a ball.

"How cool is this one?" Grant exclaimed when he saw a vessel covered with foam insulation. "It looks just like a hot dog!"

The vessel that caught Christina's eye was an ordinary-looking wooden barrel. Closer inspection revealed it was the very barrel that Annie Taylor had used.

"Look at this, Grant!" she said. "This looks a lot like the barrel that almost hit us."

"Give me a leg up, Christina," Grant said. "I want to look inside."

Peering over into the dark barrel, he couldn't believe anyone would want to crawl inside.

"Think about how cramped Annie was in this thing." Grant said. "I'll bet she felt like a sardine!"

"That was the least of their worries, Grant," Christina said, dropping her brother back to the floor. "I'm sure these daredevils were just thankful to survive!"

"I can't imagine why anyone would want to go over the falls in the first place," Grant said. "I never want to try it!"

David heard his comment. "That's a good thing, Grant," he said. "If you break the law and try a stunt at Niagara Falls, you are fined $10,000."

"Well, I can't afford to go over the falls," Grant replied. "I don't have that much money in my piggy bank."

Back at The Victoria, Ms. Bumpus had just taken sweet-smelling chocolate chip cookies out of the oven.

"Just in time!" she said cheerfully when the children burst in to the kitchen. "David, before I forget, your father called," she said. "Seems your little brother has the flu and your parents would like you to stay here with us during the rest of your autumn break. He's bringing your things by later."

"Great!" David said, excited about being able to stay with his new friends.

As they told Ms. Bumpus about their day, she became especially excited when Annie Taylor was mentioned.

"Yes!" she exclaimed. "I've always admired her for what she did with a plain old barrel, a mattress and a bicycle pump."

"Bicycle pump?" Christina questioned.

"Yes," Ms. Bumpus said. "She pumped air inside to breathe and help the barrel float."

"Ms. Bumpus?" Christina asked. "Have you ever seen any barrels in this house?"

The expression on Ms. Bumpus' face suddenly became serious. "Why would you ask that?" she questioned.

"Grant claims he found a secret room with a cat and some barrels in it," Christina answered.

"I forgot to finish telling you about Mr. Mudgers," Allison said before Ms. Bumpus could answer. "He's part Siamese, so he's very vocal."

"He talks?" Grant asked.

"No!" Allison giggled. "He meows a lot."

"Does he live here?" Christina asked.

"No, he just visits from time to time," Allison explained.

"That would explain the cat," Ms. Bumpus said. "But I don't know anything about secret rooms in this old house."

"My mom told me that The Victoria was part of the Underground Railroad," Allison said. "Many slaves from America crossed over into Canada so they couldn't be caught by bounty hunters. Maybe there was a secret room here for them to hide inside. And I'm sure some of them carried their belongings in barrels or even maybe hid in barrels themselves."

Grant's imagination started to race. "The mysterious barrels we've seen could be filled with the ghosts of those slaves who never made it to freedom," he suggested. "Ghost barrels! That's scary! David, you're bunking with me."

"I've got some good advice for each of you," Ms. Bumpus said sternly. "I wouldn't be snooping around too much."

6
SERGEANT GRANT

"Rise and shine!" Papa yelled, shaking Grant awake. "Are you ready to get started on that school report? We're going to Fort George today!"

"Yes, sir," Grant answered with a sleepy, half-hearted salute.

"I've already invited David and Allison to come along and they're having breakfast already," Papa said. "Ms. Bumpus has waffles and warm maple syrup waiting!"

"Grant, be sure to get your notebook and pen and don't forget your camera!" Mimi cautioned as they prepared to leave.

"Got everything!" Grant replied. "This will be my best report ever!"

During the drive to Fort George, Grant asked David and Allison if they'd visited the famous historical site before. "I've been there," David answered. "But it'll be cool to visit with a group of the invaders."

"What do you mean? Grant asked.

"You're Americans," Allison answered.

"So?" Grant said.

"Grant, don't you know anything about the War of 1812?" Christina asked.

"I know it was between the United States and Great Britain," he answered.

Mimi's educational radar had picked up the conversation.

"That's right, Grant," Mimi said. "But did you know that Canada was a British colony at the time? American soldiers invaded Canada during the War of 1812 to try and increase American territory. Soldiers at Fort George helped protect Canada's border from the invading Americans."

"Well, I guess the American soldiers didn't do so well," Grant said.

"They did at first," David interrupted. "Allison and I just finished studying the War of 1812 too. During the Battle of Fort George in 1813, American troops shot their cannons from

Fort Niagara on the American side of the Niagara River and destroyed most of the fort. U.S. troops captured and used the fort for seven months as a base for the U.S. troops to invade other parts of Canada. But the British troops were able to recapture the fort and it stayed in British control for the rest of the war."

"Why did the Americans, I mean we, want Fort George so badly?" Grant asked, scratching his blond head.

"Because whoever controlled the river could control supplies being transported," David answered.

"I'm impressed with how much you know, David," Christina said. "What did you make on your 1812 report?"

"An 'A'," he replied, his blue eyes twinkling as he grinned proudly.

"Well, at least I know the end of the story," Grant said. "Since we're in a foreign country right now, I know America's invasion wasn't successful!"

As Papa pulled the car into the visitor's parking area at Fort George, a loud 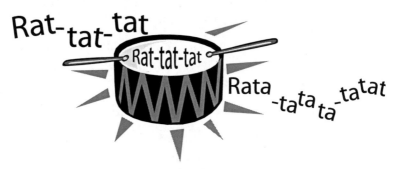echoed from the fort. "What was that?" Christina asked, startled.

"Sounds like musket fire," Allison answered.

"Cool!" Grant said, hanging his camera around his neck.

Drums sounded a steady rhythm as Papa pulled David's wheelchair from the trunk.

"Better hurry, Papa," Grant said impatiently. "It sounds like the battle's about to begin!"

As soon as they entered the fort's gates, a British soldier snapped to attention with a salute. "Are you the new **recruits**?" he asked.

Before Grant could open his mouth, Papa answered. "Yes, these are your new recruits, sir!"

Grant stared wide-eyed at Papa, who smiled and said, "Surprise! What better way to learn about the War of 1812 than to become a British soldier?"

After signing their enlistment papers, each child was given a role to play. Christina, Allison and David were regulars.

"Oh, brother!" Christina moaned when she heard Grant announced as a sergeant. "That's all I need, my little brother commanding me!"

Inside one of block houses, where soldiers would have lived and kept supplies during the War of 1812, the kids joined about ten other recruits about their age. They all slipped on their red British coats.

As a sergeant, Grant also tied a red sash with a purple stripe around his waist to signify his rank.

"Hey!" Christina remarked with a giggle. "We look sort of like the nutcrackers Mimi puts on her mantel at Christmas!"

Once again, the new soldiers heard the

Rat-tat-tat Rat-ta^{ta}$_{ta}$-ta^{tat}-ta^{tat}

of drums outside and their commanding officer barked the order, "Fall in!"

On the parade field, the recruits learned to drill in straight lines. And during a lesson on weapons used during the War of 1812, David got to fire the cannon, without a cannonball inside, of course.

Christina felt the earth tremble when the gunpowder exploded.

When Sergeant Grant got the opportunity to fire a musket, also without a musket ball, the force of the blast threw him flat on his bottom.

"Ouch!" he grumbled, rubbing his backside. "That smarted!"

During a final march around the parade ground for the watching parents and grandparents, the children passed the powder magazine, a block building where gunpowder had been kept.

"David, look!" Christina whispered. "That barrel has the same mark we saw on the barrel that almost hit us!"

As soon as the soldiers had been dismissed, Christina, Grant, David, and Allison returned to the powder magazine for a closer look at the barrel.

"Maybe there's a message inside!" Christina suggested. "Grant, why don't you climb inside and take a look?"

"That's Sergeant Grant to you, PRIVATE," Grant replied. "And salute when you speak to me!"

"Oh, yes, sir," Christina replied with a grimace. "Just climb in the barrel and look for clues."

"It's hard to see in here!" Grant's voice echoed from inside the barrel. "Anybody have a flashlight?"

"Doesn't that pen you brought have a little light in the top?" Christina asked.

"Yeah, give me that," Grant answered. His voice echoed in the barrel. "OK! I can see writing. It says:

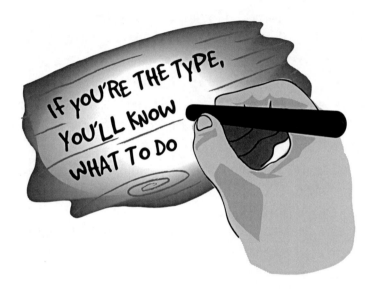

IF YOU'RE THE TYPE,
YOU'LL KNOW
WHAT TO DO

"Well, the first message we found said, JOIN THE RANKS AND ROLL," Christina said. "That's what we did today! We joined the ranks of soldiers at Fort George and it looks like that's led us to another clue! Too bad I don't have a clue what this one means!"

Reporting for duty, sir!

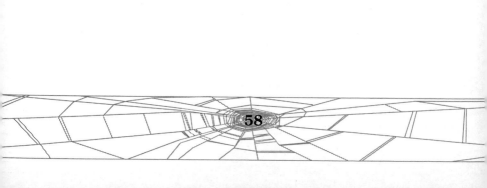

7
NEW CLUES

After an exciting morning of being a sergeant at Fort George, Mimi's plan for the afternoon sounded boring to Grant.

"A newspaper museum?" he whined. "That sounds so boring! I'd rather hang out at the falls!"

"Grant, since Mimi and Papa do so many things that we want to do, I think we should do this for them," Christina said. "Besides, we might learn something interesting."

"Okay," Grant replied. "You're right. It's Mimi and Papa's turn."

The museum, a limestone building covered with ivy, was not at all what the kids expected. It had been the home of a famous Canadian, William Lyon Mackenzie, who first published *The Colonial Advocate* in 1824 and called for an end to the colonial rule by Great Britain.

The steady, noisy clunk of machinery and the distinct smell of ink greeted them inside.

"I guess I never thought about what goes on before the newspaper gets thrown on our driveway," Christina remarked.

"Look at this!" Grant exclaimed as he examined a printing press made of wood. "It says this press was made in 1770 and is the oldest press in Canada. Wow! That's some old news!"

Christina and Allison had become fascinated with watching an antique press stamping newsprint and flipping it into a stack when Allison noticed Grant and David were missing.

"I wonder what those guys are up to," Allison said. They soon found out. David was typing on an enormous machine and Grant seemed to be telling him what to type.

"Isn't this a cool machine?" Grant asked the girls.

"What is it?" Christina asked, looking at the hundreds of moving parts.

"It's a linotype machine," David explained. "Each time I press a key, it releases a letter mold. When I get a whole line typed, it fills up the molds with hot metal that forms a 'line of type.' Get it?"

"What happens if you make a typo?" Allison asked.

"You have to throw it in this box and it gets re-melted," David explained.

"It's so hot in here, I feel like I'm melting," Christina said, wiping her brow with the back of her hand. "Allison, let's go and look at something else."

As they explored the museum looking at different wooden and metal type, something suddenly dawned on Christina. She picked up a wooden block with the letter "S" carved into it.

"Allison, what is this?" Christina asked.

"It's type of course," Allison answered.

"And what did the clue at Fort George say?" Christina asked. "IF YOU'RE THE TYPE, YOU'LL KNOW WHAT TO DO."

"Allison, I think this is the 'type' the clue was talking about!" Christina exclaimed. "That means we need to search here for another clue. Let's split up."

In a few minutes, Allison was calling to Christina. "Isn't this a strange headline for a print museum?" Allison asked, pointing to a newspaper page on a press.

DAILY NEWS

FROM NEW YORK TO GREECE, LEGO®BLOCKS ARE A BARREL OF FUN!

"Yes, that's very strange," Christina said. "Strange enough to be a clue!"

About that time, Grant came running up, with his own newspaper page in hand.

"Hot off the press!" he yelled, turning the paper around so Christina could read the headline:

DAILY NEWS

CHRISTINA HAS SMELLY FEET!

"Very funny," Christina remarked, reaching for Grant's arm as he giggled and raced back down the hall.

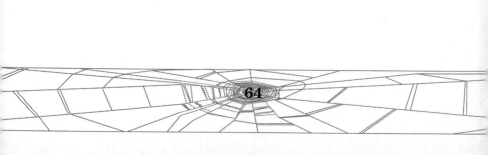

8
ROUND AND ROUND

"I call the giraffe!" Mimi yelled, running to the Loof Menagerie Carousel at Lakeside Park on Lake Ontario in Old Port Dalhousie. The family was enjoying another of Mimi's side trips.

"Wait! We have to pay first," Papa called as he fished in his pocket for change. "Can you believe this only costs a nickel?"

"That's cheap," Grant replied. "But how much is that in Canadian money?"

"Since we're so close to the American border, almost every place takes American currency, Grant," Papa explained. "But the exchange rate varies. One day an American dollar might be equal to $1.29 in Canada. On another day it could be worth only 98 cents."

"Well, I'm glad we're near the border and I don't have to do the math!" Grant said.

"I've got change for a loonie and a twoonie if you need it," David said.

"What in the world are a loonie and a twoonie?" Grant asked.

"Canadian coins that equal to a one or two dollar bill," David explained.

"Come on, David!" Grant shouted as he joined the rush to choose an animal on the magnificent antique carousel.

Although there was a spot for his wheelchair, David decided to sit this one out. "Makes me nauseous," he said.

Christina clung to the reins of a coal-black steed while Allison rode beside her on a golden palomino.

"I'm going to catch you!" Grant yelled from a muddy brown goat several animals behind them.

It was carved in a frozen stance, pawing the air as if eager to run.

"Right," Christina said. "Like a goat can catch a thoroughbred!"

As the organ-like music started to play a happy tune and the carousel lurched forward, Christina laughed at Mimi perched on her giraffe and Papa straddling a majestic lion.

David, who was thinking about the last clue, shouted "Brick!" when Christina passed and waved. On the next pass he shouted, "City!"

"What is he talking about?" Christina asked Allison. "What is Brick City?"

Allison said excitedly. "I bet that's where we find our next clue."

After the carousel ride, Mimi, dizzy from going round and round, suggested a traditional Canadian treat – maple syrup over snow.

"Where do they get the snow?" Grant asked. "I haven't seen any snow."

"Nowadays, it's served over finely crushed ice," Allison explained.

"Too sweet for me!" Grant exclaimed after a few licks. "I'll stick to syrup on my pancakes."

"You make such a mess when you eat pancakes, you usually do stick to something!" Christina teased.

"Papa, could we visit Brick City before we return to The Victoria?" Christina asked. "It has all sorts of famous places like the Statue of Liberty made out of LEGO blocks."

Now it was Mimi's turn to be bored. "You've seen the real thing!" she said. "Why would you want to see the Statue of Liberty made out of little plastic blocks?"

9
PLASTIC PLACES

Inside Brick City, Christina quickly wondered if she'd made the wrong decision. The place was packed with so many little kids, it was hard to concentrate on searching for clues.

"I see the torch," Allison said, pointing over the heads of preschoolers.

"Remember," Christina reminded, "the clue said: 'FROM NEW YORK TO GREECE, LEGO BLOCKS ARE A BARREL OF FUN.' So we should look for something associated with Greece."

Winding their way around the many structures made from the plastic blocks, Christina spotted something she'd seen in her history book.

"It's the Acropolis!" she shouted. "That's in Greece. If there is a clue, it should be around here somewhere."

"I'm going over here to make something," Grant said.

"Grant, you should be looking for clues!" Christina scolded.

"I won't be long," Grant promised. "But I can't resist those barrels overflowing with every kind of LEGO imaginable."

"Did you say barrels?" Christina asked.

"Yep," he answered. "Over there."

Grabbing her brother's sleeve, she pulled him toward the barrels. To their surprise, one of the barrels bore the same mysterious mark as the other barrels that had contained clues.

Christina and Allison started scooping out building blocks and scattering them on one of the project tables where kids could build their own creations. David rolled up to the table and Grant pulled up a chair alongside him.

"Aren't you guys going to help?" Christina asked.

"There's not room around that barrel for all of us," Grant said. "Besides, we're supposed to be on vacation, not just clue hunting."

"I think I see something!" Christina said excitedly.

Building blocks spilled everywhere as Christina leaned too far over, tipping the barrel. When two Brick City staffers helped her to her feet, Christina was red-faced, but smiling.

"Got it!" she said triumphantly.

"Got what?" David asked, as he put the finishing touches on a replica of Maid of the Mist.

"I found another clue!" Christina said, pulling a piece of wrinkled paper out of the barrel.

GRAPES WHINE
SO PEOPLE
CAN DINE.

"Sounds like a weird clue," David said. "Are you sure we're really on the right track?"

10

WHINE OR DINE?

"I'm hungry!" Grant announced as they drove back to the town of Niagara Falls.

"Look at this gorgeous sunset!" Mimi exclaimed, as she ignored Grant and admired the golden glow on the horizon.

"Papa, we are going to get something to eat before we get back to The Victoria aren't we?" Grant asked. "You know we haven't had a bite since that ice with the syrup on top. How much farther is it back into town where all the restaurants are?"

Papa had heard enough. "Grant, we are going to get something to eat," he said. "But I really don't want 'whine' with my dinner."

"I know a great place that makes delicious chili and also has an oxygen bar," David suggested.

"What is an oxygen bar?" Grant asked. "Doesn't sound very filling."

"It's a place where you pay to breathe pure oxygen," David explained. "It even comes in different scents like peppermint. Some people think it gives them more energy."

"Chili sounds good," Papa said. "But I think we'll stick to breathing plain old everyday oxygen for free."

Inside the restaurant, Christina noticed the red-haired deckhand from the *Maid of the Mist* seated at the oxygen bar. He had plastic tubes in his nose like a hospital patient and was chatting with one of the restaurant employees as he breathed in pure oxygen.

"Breathing all that Niagara Falls mist probably keeps his head stuffy," she said. "Guess the oxygen helps."

After two bowls of steaming chili, Grant finally announced he was full. Christina was thumbing through a visitor's guide when she noticed an article about the region's vineyards.

"I didn't know they grow grapes here," she said to Allison.

"Yes," Allison replied. "That's one of the things the Niagara region is known for."

Christina began thinking again about the last strange clue she'd found.

"Allison," she said. "Don't they put wine in barrels?"

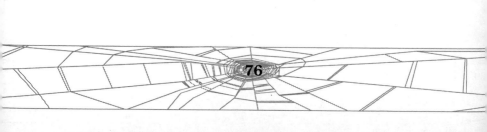

11

COWBOYS AND CANADIANS

After Christina had shown Mimi and Papa the beautiful pictures of the vineyards around the Niagara Falls region, it was easy for them to decide what the next day's adventure would be: Puddicombe Estate Farms and Winery.

"Help!" Grant yelled, as everyone else boarded the little train for a ride around the farm.

A grumpy goose with his neck stretched and wings spread wide chased Grant as he ran in circles to escape.

"Yesterday you were a brave sergeant and now you're afraid of a sweet little ol' goose!" Christina teased.

"Move over! Make room for me!" Grant cried, diving head first into his train seat. "That goose is mean, not sweet!"

As the little train chugged around the farm, Christina was amazed at the rows of grape vines and fruit trees, now clothed in autumn colors, standing in perfect lines like dutiful soldiers.

At the farm's general store everyone enjoyed a lunch of cheese and freshly harvested pears.

"Do you still put wine in barrels here?" Christina asked the storekeeper.

"No," he answered. "The winery was moved to another location several years ago, but there are still a few outbuildings with barrels in them. Not much to see."

Christina whispered to Allison, "Well, there might be something for us to see!"

"We're going to buy some fresh-picked apples," Mimi said. "Do you want to come along?"

"I think we'd like to do some exploring," Christina said as the other children nodded in agreement.

"Just stay in this area," Mimi ordered.

As soon as Mimi and Papa walked away, they all headed for an old shed.

"David, why you don't wait here at the corner, and if you see anyone coming, give us a signal," Christina suggested.

"What will the signal be?" David asked.

"Why don't you whistle?" Grant suggested. "You know, just like cowboys and Indians."

"More like cowboys and Canadians," David chuckled.

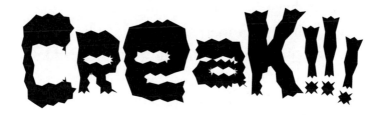

The shed door creaked loudly when Christina pulled on it. "Give me your pen light," Christina told Grant as she peered into the darkness.

"Yep, I see lots of old barrels," she said. "I wonder if any of them have the mark all the other clue barrels have had?"

"Christina, look!" Grant said. "Third one from the top."

As they examined the mark, Christina heard a muffled sneeze.

"Did one of you just sneeze?" she asked Grant and Allison.

"Wasn't me," Allison said.

"Me, either," Grant said.

"That sounds like it's coming from inside the barrel!" Christina said.

She gingerly tapped a rhythm on the barrel's side. Surprisingly, something inside repeated the same rhythm.

"Quick!" Christina commanded. "Let's get this lid off this barrel!"

Grant spotted a crow bar hanging on the wall and the three of them pried off the top.

Look at all these barrels!

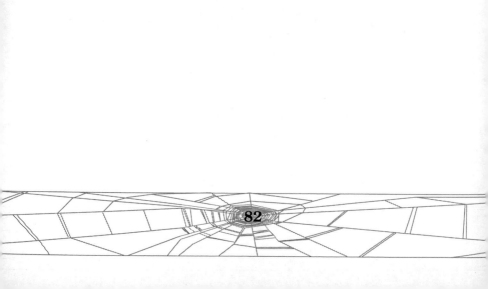
82

When Christina shined the light inside the barrel, the first thing she saw was red hair!

With panic in his eyes, a young red-haired man pulled himself out of the barrel and darted for the door.

"What happened?" Christina yelled. "Who put you in that barrel?"

Without looking back, the man cried, "Be careful around the green water!" A loud whistle from David let them know he had rounded the corner of the shed.

"Did you see his face?" Christina asked David, as the kids raced to David's side.

"No," he answered. "All I noticed was a blur of red hair."

12

HYDRO HEAVEN

"I have to say these clues have me stumped," Christina said softly. She didn't want Mimi and Papa to hear as they drove to the Sir Adam Beck Generating Station for a tour.

"Yeah," Grant whispered. "We've had no trouble finding clues, but they don't seem to be leading us anywhere. We're just going from clue to clue."

"Well," David said, "the redhead mentioned water and that's where we're headed. Maybe we'll find the answer, or at least another clue."

"Sure hope you're right," Christina said. "I just want to know if that first barrel was aimed at me, or if I just happened to be in the way."

"Hey, Papa," Grant said. "You just passed through the town of Niagara Falls. I thought we were going to the generating station."

"We are, Grant," he replied. "It's actually downstream from Niagara Falls."

"Who is Sir Adam Beck, anyway?" Grant asked.

"We studied him in school," Allison said. "He was knighted by King George V."

"You have knights in Canada?" Grant asked, impressed.

"Not the kind who ride horses and wear armor," David laughed.

"Usually, someone is knighted for doing good service or great deeds for his or her country," Mimi explained. "Sir Adam Beck believed that Niagara's great water resources should be used to provide affordable electricity for the people of this area, not just the rich people. He became known as the Power Minister."

"How'd you know that, Mimi?" Grant asked.

"I'm reading straight from the brochure," Mimi said with a grin.

The power station was amazingly quiet compared to the roar of Niagara Falls. As they looked cautiously from an observation area to the bottom of the dam, they could see that the water was gurgling from underneath.

"Not what you expected?" a tour guide asked.

"Not exactly," Grant answered.

"Why wasn't the power plant built closer to the falls?" Christina asked.

"Niagara was chosen because it had more falling water than any other place and was the best place to build a power facility," the guide said. "But, it required the area with the highest drop and surprisingly, it wasn't at the falls. It was five miles down river here at Queenstown where the cliffs are more than twice as high.

"When the power plant was built in 1917," he continued, "it was the largest power station in the world. Sir Adam Beck himself flipped the switch and the power lit up a sign that said, 'For the People'."

"It's so old that I'm surprised it can still make electricity," Grant said.

"It works pretty much the same as it did back then," the guide explained. "Water comes through a pipe over the cliff and when it's released at the bottom it turns a propeller, or turbine. The propeller drives a shaft that makes electromagnets spin and create electricity. In the beginning, there were only two generators. Now there are ten. But, if the Niagara River stops flowing, our lights will still go out!"

"Christina, don't you dare go near those magnets," Grant warned.

"Why not?" Christina asked.

"It could draw your braces to it and then your mouth would be stuck to the generator!" he cried, with a big belly laugh.

"You know, you'll probably get braces in a year or two," Christina said. "It'll be payback time for me then!"

"What is that other giant wall of concrete I see down there?" Grant asked, pointing his skinny arm to the opposite side of the cliffs.

"That's Sir Adam Beck Number II," the guide said. "After World War II, people needed more electricity, so another power plant was built.

Water for that plant is taken from the upper Niagara River and brought here through two huge tunnels that run under the City of Niagara Falls. The tunnels are more than five miles long!"

"I'm surprised there's any water left to come over Niagara Falls," Christina said.

"That's a good point, Christina," the guide said. "Since both the Canadians and Americans were using Niagara's water, people became afraid the falls would be reduced to a little trickle. So the United States and Canada signed an agreement to protect the beauty of the falls.

"The plan limits the water taken from the river between 8 a.m. and 10 p.m. during the tourist season, April to October," he continued. "At night, extra water goes into reservoirs to be used during the day."

"I'm glad," Grant said. "I would have been really mad if I came to Niagara Falls and only saw a trickle!"

"How about one more stop before we call it day?" Papa asked with enthusiasm after they'd toured the power station. "How'd you guys like to see some ships climb a mountain?"

"Are you trying to be funny, Papa?" Grant asked.

"I'm serious," Papa said. "Get in the car and I'll show you!"

After they stopped at the Lock 3 viewing platform at the Welland Canals, Grant was still skeptical.

"OK, Papa," he said. "You've got some explaining to do."

"Sometimes boats need to go from Lake Ontario to Lake Erie," Papa said, pulling out a map. "See, the Niagara River connects those lakes along the U.S. and Canada border. The problem is that Lake Erie is 327 feet higher than Lake Ontario and boats can't jump. These canals and locks were built to help the boats go up to Lake Erie or go down to Lake Ontario."

"Hmmm," Grant said, scratching his blond head.

"Just think about the *Maid of the Mist*," Papa continued. "Remember when it's at the bottom of Niagara Falls and how far it is to the top of Niagara Falls? It has no way to get up there unless it goes through locks."

"Oh look!" Christina pointed. "Here comes a big ship!"

"It doesn't look like it's going to fit into the lock," Grant observed, as the ship slowly made its way up the canal.

"It has just enough room," Papa said, as the ship eased between the concrete walls.

"Look how far down it is," Grant said.

"Watch what happens when those giant gates close behind the ship," Mimi said.

Slowly, the ship began to rise and soon the ship's bottom was almost even with the top of the concrete walls.

"That reminds me of when I watch my rubber ducky rise to the top when I fill up the bathtub," Grant said.

"You have a rubber ducky?" David asked.

"And you admit it?" Allison laughed.

"Hey," Grant replied, "it's a cool duck!"

When the gates in front of the ship opened, it pulled out of the lock.

"That was cool, Papa," Grant said. "Now I understand how ships can climb mountains."

"How many locks are there between the two lakes, Papa?" Christina asked.

"Seven in all," he answered. "It takes ships about 12 hours to go through all the locks from one lake to the other and more than a thousand make the trip each year. I read that this system was first built in the early 1800s. Of course, it's been improved many times since then."

"Thank goodness it's not going to take us 12 hours to get back to Niagara Falls," Grant said. "I'm starved."

Christina was more **perplexed** than hungry. She had noticed the water was green at the power station and inside the locks. David said dissolved minerals gave the water its color.

Weren't they supposed to be careful around green water?

13

LIQUID COLOR

The sun had set by the time they arrived back in Niagara Falls but the colorful signs of the town's entertainment district, Clifton Hill, electrified the night sky.

Somehow, Christina and Grant hadn't noticed the giant Ferris wheel before now. "That's the biggest Ferris wheel I've ever seen!" Grant said.

"That's the Niagara Sky Wheel," David announced.

"Can we ride it, Papa?" Grant begged. "PLEEEEEEEESE!!"

"I thought you were starving," Papa remarked, tousling Grants' blond curls.

"Dinner can wait!" Grant said.

Mimi agreed. "Good idea, Grant," she said. "That giant Ferris wheel is probably best on an empty stomach. You know how you sometimes get motion sickness."

When Mimi and Papa climbed into their own gondola, Grant was confused.

"Don't you want to ride with us?" he asked.

"Papa and I want to enjoy the romantic view alone," Mimi said.

"Awwww," Christina said. "Look at the honeymooners!"

The kids waited for a handicap-accessible gondola to come around so David could join them. The night air was chilly, but inside the gondola a heater kept them warm and cozy.

The giant wheel slowly lifted them above the bright lights of Clifton Hill. As they reached the top, the most spectacular sight of all came into view. Both the Horseshoe Falls and the American Falls were awash in beautiful colors coming from powerful spotlights across the gorge.

"It's beautiful liquid color," Christina exclaimed.

As she stared at the American Falls closest to them, Christina couldn't help but notice Bridal Veil Falls, separated by an island of rock from the main portion of the American Falls. It was bathed in green light.

"Could that be the green water we were warned about?" Christina asked.

"It looks greenest at the Cave of the Winds at the base of Bridal Veil Falls," David replied.

"What's the Cave of the Winds?" Grant asked.

"It used to be a real cave," David explained. "But after it collapsed in the 1950s, people were afraid it was no longer safe to go inside, so they used dynamite to close it up. Now, there's a wooden walkway down to the bottom of Bridal Veil Falls, where you get to see it up close."

"I've been there," Allison said. "It's like being inside a hurricane."

Christina knew she had to find out if this was the answer to the clue. When the skywheel stopped and they joined Mimi and Papa, she asked Mimi, "Don't you think it would be beautiful to see the falls up close at night?"

"I do, dear," she said. "But I'm beat."

"Well, would you mind if we visited the Cave of the Winds?" Christina asked. "You and Papa can rest and then maybe we can get some burgers to eat later."

Mimi didn't have time to answer before Papa butted in. "Sounds good to me," he said. "Here's some money for your tickets and some extra just in case you need it," he said, pulling out his wallet. "We'll drive you across the Rainbow Bridge to the American side and make sure a tour guide is in charge of you. We'll be waiting outside. Make sure you all stay together!"

14

WET WIND

"The hottest fashion accessory in Niagara Falls is yellow plastic," Christina said, as she slipped on a souvenir plastic raincoat for the Cave of the Winds tour.

"I'm keeping these plastic shoe covers to wear in the shower on the mornings I'm late to school," Grant said. "Then I can take a shower in my shoes and save some time."

"Great idea," Christina said, shaking her head at her brother's silly idea.

"Is everyone ready?" asked a guide in a bright red rain suit.

"Good thing Mimi's not here," Christina said. "She'd want a red suit like that to match her red boots!"

As an elevator took them down 175 feet, Grant said impatiently, "This is the longest elevator ride I've ever taken!"

The elevator doors opened to reveal Bridal Veil Falls decked out in her evening color.

"We're about 150 feet away from the base of Bridal Veil Falls," the guide shouted over the thunderous racket of the falls. "If you'd like to get even closer, follow me."

Grant immediately fell in line behind the guide and was already several steps down the wooden walkway when he realized no one else was with him. He felt terrible when he saw that Allison and Christina were standing beside David in his wheelchair, which couldn't make the rest of the journey.

Running back to apologize, he begged David's forgiveness. "I'm sorry, David, I forgot," Grant said.

"No reason to apologize," David responded cheerfully. "I'd like to stay here and watch people go by while you go the rest of the way. You never know what I might see or hear. You all better get going. The guide's leaving you!"

"It does look like a bride's flowing veil!" Christina observed as they made their way to the bottom of Bridal Veil Falls. Mini waterfalls and streams raced along the rocky cliff beside the walkway and huge rocks at the base made the water explode into tiny droplets that formed an eerie, colorful mist.

As they neared the Hurricane Deck, Grant began to second guess his decision.

"That looks pretty intense," he yelled, watching those in front of him turn their backs to the soaking spray.

"Are you turning chicken?" Christina shouted over the noise.

"No way!" he shouted back.

Grant cinched his plastic hood until only his eyes and nose were visible.

"I'm ready," he said, bracing himself against the rail.

Christina and Allison also leaned into the powerful wind and spray coming off the falling water. Christina tried to focus on looking for clues in the green water.

Holding the rail tightly, she squinted and wiped the water from her eyes. Still, the water was a blur as the icy cold water droplets hit Christina's face like needles.

"Did you see anything?" Christina yelled as they left the Hurricane Deck.

"I was too busy surviving!" Grant shouted. "Now I know why it's important to get out of town when a hurricane's coming!"

As soon as they reached the spot on the walkway where they could see David, he looked like he was watching for them. When he saw them, he waved his arms wildly.

"Hurry!" he shouted.

15

TUNNEL TALES

"What is it?" Christina gasped when she reached David.

"I overheard two people talking about barrels and gold and a plan," David exclaimed.

"What did they look like?" Christina asked.

"I couldn't see their faces," he said. "One of them was a woman with curly brown hair. The other was a man wearing a yellow raincoat."

"David, everyone here is wearing a yellow raincoat!" Christina reminded him.

"No, it wasn't one of these thin plastic ones," David explained. "It was a real raincoat."

"What did they say?" Christina asked.

"I couldn't make out everything over the noise of the falls," he said. "Something about the gold in barrels being a good plan."

"Did they say anything else?" Christina asked.

"One more thing," David replied. "They said the Horseshoe tunnels would be best."

"There are tunnels cut through the rock behind the Horseshoe Falls!" Allison said.

"Let's go!" Christina shouted.

Rushing back across the Rainbow Bridge, the kids purchased tickets for a Journey Behind the Falls to explore the tunnels. They were thankful Papa had given them extra money.

Another elevator ride opened to tunnels that shimmered with the mist coming off the white sheet of water visible through small, window-like openings.

The noise of the falls inside the tunnels sounded like the static from a radio with the volume on high.

"Look at this!" Christina exclaimed, as she dashed into a side tunnel to find several empty barrels, a coil of plastic tubing, and an oxygen tank.

"How strange!" she remarked. Before she could say anything else, she heard a gruff voice coming from a shadowy figure she hadn't noticed.

"You kids need to get out of here before you get into trouble!" the voice yelled.

Christina didn't need to be told twice. She knew they were in a dangerous position alone in the tunnels.

"Go!" she yelled to the others. "Let's get out of here!"

As they ran, with David leading the way in his wheelchair, Christina could hear heavy footsteps behind them.

"FASTER!"

she yelled breathlessly. "I think he's gaining on us!"

Watching in horror, Christina saw Grant slip and fall hard on the slippery tunnel floor.

David heard Christina yell and spun his chair around. "Keep running!" he bellowed to Christina and Allison. "I'll get him!"

As Grant struggled to his feet, David pulled him onto his lap, and rolled his chair as fast as he could.

Christina could see the elevator ahead. If only they could make it inside! She yanked Allison's arm and pulled her inside the elevator's open doors, scrambling to find the button to hold the doors open until Grant and David were safely inside too.

As soon as David's chair cleared the door, Christina pushed the close button.

"Whew!" Christina gasped, collapsing against the elevator wall.

"CHRISTINA, WATCH OUT!"

Allison screamed as she watched an arm covered by a heavy yellow raincoat reach in to block the elevator doors just before they shut. But, startled by the pressure of the closing doors, their pursuer yanked his arm out and the doors shut completely.

When the doors opened on the surface, the kids were relieved to see Mimi and Papa standing there waiting for them.

"You're late!" Papa said. "You were supposed to be at our meeting place 10 minutes ago!"

"How'd you know we were here?" Grant asked.

"I know how your minds work," Papa said with a frown.

16

HOT CHOCOLATE, HOT GOLD

Christina closed her eyes and concentrated on the hot chocolate flowing down her throat, bringing much needed warmth to her chilled body.

Ms. Bumpus gave each of them a blanket warmed in the dryer to make them even cozier as they warmed by the crackling fire in the stone fireplace.

Ms. Bumpus noticed Christina staring at the bottom of her skirt, which was wet and had pieces of grass stuck to it. "Do you think this firewood walked in here by itself?" she asked with a smile. "The mist was blowing from the falls this afternoon and the grass is damp."

"They were talking about gold," David said, rehashing the night's events after Ms Bumpus left the room. "I've heard a tale about gold here in Niagara."

"Tell us!" Grant said.

"Have you ever heard of Laura Secord?" David asked.

"The chocolate lady?" Christina asked.

"The chocolate brand was named for her," David said, "but she was famous for something else. During the War of 1812, three American soldiers invaded her homestead. She overheard them talking about a surprise attack on British forces.

"She made up a story for the Americans," he continued, "about going to visit her brother, but instead walked 20 miles to warn British forces about the American plans. Thanks to what she did, the attack never happened and the Niagara area remained a part of Canada."

"Do you mean if it hadn't been for Laura we'd be in the United States right now instead of Canada?" Grant asked.

"That's right!" David said.

"But what about gold?" Christina asked.

"Well, when Laura was 85 years old, the Prince of Wales gave her a reward for what she did," David explained. "Some stories say it was only 100 pounds."

"One hundred pounds of what?" Grant interrupted.

"British pounds," David explained. "That's what British money is called.

"Anyway," David continued, "another story is that Laura Secord knew of hidden gold from the War of 1812! One legend says that an old hermit named Francis Abbot who lived on Goat Island found the gold and hid it there."

"Where is Goat Island?" Grant asked.

"That's the piece of land that lies between the American Falls and Horseshoe Falls," Allison explained.

"What a beautiful place to live!" Christina exclaimed, as she imagined living right beside one of the world's most famous landmarks. "I guess it would be lonely, though."

"They say he entertained tourists by balancing on a wooden pier over the rapids," David said. "He died while bathing in the Niagara River in 1831 and the truth about his gold was never known."

"He was taking a bath when he lived right next to Niagara Falls, the biggest shower on earth?" Grant joked.

"What if it wasn't a legend?" David suggested. "What if someone has found the old hermit's gold and they're trying to smuggle it from the island?"

Ms. Bumpus entered the room with an odd look on her face.

"You kids ought not to concern yourselves with such things," she scowled. "It'll make you have bad dreams. Forget about legends and gold and keep your noses out of business that isn't yours!"

Three cups of hot chocolate had Grant's mind on something else.

"Be right back," he said, running to the restroom in his room upstairs.

On his way out of the restroom, Grant heard a noise. Stopping in his tracks to listen, he heard a muffled, "meow, meow, meow."

"Must be Mr. Mudgers," Grant said to himself. As he passed the fireplace wall, he was surprised to see a small crack.

"I'll prove to Christina I wasn't making it up," Grant said, pushing as the wall slowly creaked opened wide enough for him to enter the secret room.

Grant ran to the top of the stairs and yelled down at his sister. "Christina! Come here quick!"

When Christina reached the room, Grant said, "Look, I told you I wasn't making up the secret room!"

"There are barrels in here!" Christina said, amazed. Spying some candles, she walked over and felt one.

"Grant, these candles are still warm!" she said. "Whoever was using them is probably still around!"

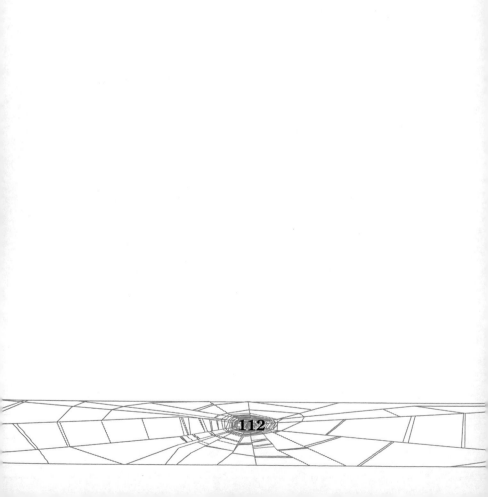

17

FLOATING GOLD

"This is our last day of sightseeing," Mimi said sadly the next morning at breakfast. "I'd like to spend an hour or so at the Butterfly Conservatory this morning. You know how much I love butterflies and the Conservatory has 50 different species."

"They'll probably think your red hat is a rose," Christina said, giggling.

The Butterfly Conservatory was only a short drive away, but Christina felt she had stepped into a tropical rainforest when she entered the giant greenhouse on the grounds of the Niagara Parks Botanical Garden.

Butterflies floated on the warm, moist air like colorful snowflakes among the exotic plants.

"I didn't know there were so many different kinds of butterflies!" Grant said, as he watched a purple butterfly and a brown spotted butterfly, sipping nectar from a beautiful white peace lily taller than his head.

"I told you it would happen," Christina laughed, pointing at Mimi's red hat where a large red butterfly was hitching a ride. Papa's brown cowboy hat looked festive with several colorful butterflies mistaking Papa for a tall flower.

"Quick, take my picture," Allison told Christina after a small green butterfly landed right on her nose.

When David stopped along the winding path to admire the waterfall inside the conservatory, butterflies seemed attracted to his black hair.

"How cute!" Christina said when she saw the butterfly nursery. Eggs, larvae, and cocoons shared the cage with butterflies that had just begun to fly.

"Time to join your friends," a conservatory worker said as she opened a window to set free the newly emerged golden butterflies.

Don't Sneeze!

"That's gold that floats!" the worker said.

Golden butterflies float on the air, but real gold is too heavy to float on water, Christina thought, as her mind drifted to the legendary gold.

"Or is it?" she whispered softly to herself.

"Who's brave enough for a trip over the Niagara Gorge in the Whirlpool Aero Car?" Papa asked as they left the conservatory.

"We are!" the kids said in unison.

But during the drive to the Niagara Gorge, Christina couldn't stop thinking about the floating gold.

"How could you make something as heavy as gold float?" Christina asked the others.

"You could put it on a boat," Grant said.

"What if it needed to float where it was too dangerous for a boat to go?" Christina asked.

"Maybe you could put it inside a balloon." David remarked.

"Or a barrel!" Christina said.

"Do you remember what Annie Taylor did with a bicycle pump?" Christina asked. "She pumped air into a barrel to help it float! These days if someone wanted to put air into a barrel, they'd probably just use an oxygen tank like the one we saw in the tunnels."

"How would you keep the air from leaking out?" Allison asked.

"You'd have to seal it with something," Grant said. "Something like the wax from the candles in the secret room!"

"That's it!" Christina exclaimed. "Someone is taking the gold from Goat Island, sealing it in barrels filled with oxygen to go over the falls and down the river!"

"But who?" David asked.

As Mimi, Papa, and the kids boarded the historic red aero car for a trip over the gorge, Grant had second thoughts.

"I just read a sign that said this cable car was built in 1916!" he said. "I'm not sure I want to ride on something that old."

"Don't worry, it's been updated since then," David said. "Besides, it's the only way to get a bird's eye view of the whirlpool."

As the aero car crawled slowly along the cable high above the basin surrounded by cliffs, Grant observed, "This looks like a big cereal bowl."

"I see the whirlpool," Christina said. "It looks like a tornado in the water."

"What makes it do that?" Grant asked.

"The water enters the basin fast and as it travels counterclockwise, it cuts across itself and causes the water to spin," Mimi explained. "Sort of the way the water looks when you rinse out your cereal bowl."

"I sure would hate to fall in," Allison said.

"Me too," Grant said. "I read on the sign that it's 126 feet deep."

Christina, leaning over the edge of the car studying the whirlpool below, suddenly shouted, "What's that? It looks like a big cork being sucked into the whirlpool. Grant, give me your binoculars."

"That's no cork!" said Grant, already looking. "That's a barrel!"

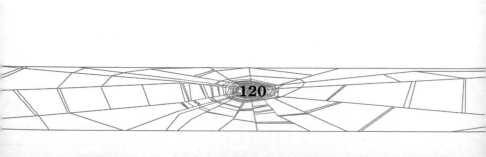

18

THUNDER OF WATERS

"Is there any way to get closer to the whirlpool?" Christina asked David.

"The whirlpool jet boats go right through it," David answered.

It was easy for Christina and Grant to convince Papa to let them take a tour on the Wet Jet to the whirlpool.

"Sounds like fun!" he said.

This time, instead of raincoats, entire wetsuits were provided for what Christina was sure would be a drenching experience.

"We look like frogmen!" Grant said, giggling as they zipped on the suits.

As soon as the Wet Jet fired its powerful engines, Christina knew it was going to be a wild, wet ride. The force of the takeoff pressed her back against the seat and she looked at David who was hanging on for dear life.

Soon, a steady spray was covering them each time the boat hit a wake.

"Thank goodness for wetsuits," Mimi said, gripping her seat as they bobbed up and down along the rapids.

As the boat entered the whirlpool basin, Christina found the rushing water's fury frightening.

"Now I know why the Indians named it Niagara," Allison yelled.

"What does it mean?" Christina shouted back.

"Thunder of the waters," she replied.

"My hat!" Mimi screamed as she watched her red hat fly over the back of the boat and land on the outer edges of the whirlpool.

Papa quickly removed his cowboy hat and stuffed it under his seat.

They watched the red hat make several circles around the whirlpool and then disappear in its center.

"Sorry, Mimi!" Christina said. Turning to David, she added, "Guess that's what happened to the barrel too!"

But just as the Wet Jet turned to return to the dock, a flash of yellow from a small clearing in a grove of trees caught Christina's eye. She wondered if it was a yellow raincoat!

"David, we've got to get to that clearing!" she said.

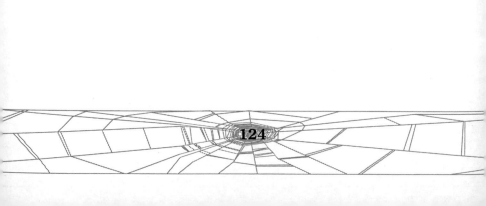

19

REDHEAD HERRINGS

"We'll be right back!" Christina promised as they peeled off their wet suits.

"Make sure you are!" Papa yelled after the four of them as they dashed down a path along the shore.

Christina warned as they cautiously approached the edge of the clearing.

"Grant, take a look through your binoculars," Christina whispered.

"Do you see anything?" she asked.

"It's a guy in a yellow raincoat," he said. "And you're not going to believe this – a woman in a long black skirt!"

"Give me those binoculars," Christina said. She watched as the man and woman worked to pull a barrel onto the shore. "Careful, son!" she heard the woman shout.

"The barrel's got the same mark as all the others!" Christina said. "This has got to be the end of our clue trail!"

Quietly, Christina pulled the camera out of her pocket to take a picture for the authorities. At the same time, a gnat flew into Grant's nose.

"AHHHH CHOO!"

he sneezed loudly.

Quickly the man and woman spun around so that Christina could see their faces.

She recognized the man as the deckhand from the Maid of the Mist. She also recognized the woman in the long black skirt.

"It's Ms. Bumpus!" Christina exclaimed.

"I heard something," Ms. Bumpus told the man. "Check over there," she ordered, pointing straight at where Christina and the others were hidden.

"We better get out of here!" Christina cried, as she motioned for the others to head back down the path to the safety of the dock.

As she rounded a sharp curve in the path, Christina ran right into a startled, red-haired young man. It was the same red-haired young man they had pulled from the barrel at Puddicombe Farms! But this time he was wearing a uniform.

"Who are you?" Christina asked.

"I'm Detective Roberts with the Niagara Parks Police," he answered. "Are you OK?"

"We think there are gold thieves are in the clearing!" she said.

Detective Roberts was radioing for backup as Christina watched him run back toward the clearing.

When the kids returned to the clearing to see what was happening, Ms. Bumpus and her son were being led away in handcuffs.

Detective Roberts was using a crowbar to open the barrel.

"Sorry I couldn't talk to you guys before now," he said when he saw the kids.

"I suspected something strange was going on with barrels after several sightings were reported. Then I saw the barrel almost hit you when I was off duty," he told Christina.

"I was investigating reports of missing barrels at Puddicombe Farms," the detective continued, "when several people forced me into the barrel. I don't know what I would have done if you hadn't come along. I didn't want to get you involved, but I did want to warn you that they were talking about the green water."

"I'm glad this mystery is solved," Christina told Detective Roberts. "Instead of red herrings, there were redheads! I thought you were one of the bad guys!"

The barrel lid flew off and landed on the ground.

"Meow, meow, meow."

"What is that?" a surprised Detective Roberts asked.

"It's Mr. Mudgers!" Allison exclaimed. "I'd know that meow anywhere."

A very dizzy Siamese cat climbed slowly out of the barrel.

"I guess poor Mr. Mudgers was napping in this barrel when they sealed it in the secret room at The Victoria," Grant said.

Peering into the barrel, Detective Roberts exclaimed, "There's a gold bar inside too!"

20

FALLING FOR HISTORY

On the way back to The Victoria, Christina and Grant told a surprised Mimi and Papa about their Niagara Falls mystery.

Allison's surprise was finding her mother waiting at the front door.

"Did you hear about Ms. Bumpus?" Allison asked.

"Yes, I'm afraid Ms. Bumpus won't be working here anymore," Mrs. Cooper said. "She and her son confessed to stealing gold from park property on Goat Island and illegally sending barrels over Niagara Falls."

"I didn't even know Ms. Bumpus had a son," Allison said.

"Neither did I," Mrs. Cooper replied. "The good thing is that now the gold has been found, it will be used to maintain the parks."

"Why did Ms. Bumpus and her son want the gold?" Grant asked.

"They were a group of people who reenacted parts of the War of 1812," Mrs. Cooper explained. "They came up with a plan to start a tour boat company to compete with the *Maid of the Mist.*"

"Is that why Ms. Bumpus wore clothes that looked like they were from the 1800s?" David asked.

"Yes," Mrs. Cooper replied. "The police said they had even stamped the crest of their regiment on barrels that they used to hide gold and communicate plans."

"So that was the strange mark on all those barrels!" Christina said.

Allison had another question on her mind.

"Mom, do you think I could keep Mr. Mudgers as a pet?" she asked, stroking the purring cat's head. "You know he doesn't belong to anyone and he needs a forever home."

"Where would he stay?" Mrs. Cooper asked.

"I know the perfect little hideaway," Grant said with a smile.

Christina noticed that David had a sad expression on face. "What's wrong?" she asked.

"I wish you didn't have to go back to Georgia," he answered. "It's been fun touring Niagara with you."

"I know," Grant said. "I wouldn't mind invading Canada again sometime."

"Why don't you come back in July for Friendship Festival?" Allison suggested.

"What's that?" Christina asked.

"It's a celebration of the shared history and friendship between the United States and Canada," Allison answered.

"Maybe we can plan that," Papa said. "Grant can give a speech on the War of 1812!"

"We'd love to come back," Mimi agreed. "I think Niagara Falls is a barrel of fun!"

Well, that was fun!

Wow, glad we solved that mystery!

Where shall we go next?

EVERYWHERE!

The End

Now...go to
www.carolemarshmysteries.com
and...

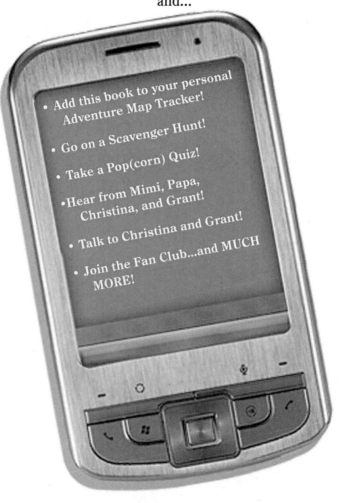

- Add this book to your personal Adventure Map Tracker!

- Go on a Scavenger Hunt!

- Take a Pop(corn) Quiz!

- Hear from Mimi, Papa, Christina, and Grant!

- Talk to Christina and Grant!

- Join the Fan Club...and MUCH MORE!

BUILT-IN BOOK CLUB

TALK ABOUT IT!

1. If you could have your own Victorian home, what would it look like? Would there be any secret rooms?

2. Have you ever been to Niagara Falls? If not, would you ever want to go? Which place from the book would you most like to visit?

3. If you lived a hundred years ago, would you have tried to be a daredevil and go down the falls in a barrel?

4. Who was your favorite character in the book? Why?

5. Grant, Christina, Allison and David were in a war re-enactment. Have you ever been in a re-enactment of anything in history? If so, what did you re-enact and what role did you play?

6. Would you be brave enough to go on the Hurricane Deck?

7. If you could build a replica of anything out of LEGO blocks, what would it be?

8. What was your favorite part of the book? Why?

BUILT-IN BOOK CLUB

BRING IT TO LIFE!

1. It is a Canadian tradition to eat maple syrup over snow. In the book, Grant and Christina try maple syrup over ice. As a book club, get some shaved ice and maple syrup and try it! See what other treats you can make up with shaved ice!

2. Have members of your book club bring in as many LEGO blocks as they can. Build a replica of a famous place or building or even create your own LEGO block city.

3. Research Niagara Falls and the different attractions surrounding it. Plan your dream trip to the falls!

4. Use the Internet to see what the current exchange rates are for American currency in Canada. If you only have a dollar, is it worth more in America or Canada?

5. Have each member of the book club draw what their dream Victorian home would look like. Would you have any secret rooms? If so, what would you put in there?

GLOSSARY

conservatory: a greenhouse for growing or displaying plants and animals

erosion: the process by which the surface of the earth is worn away by water

gondola: an enclosed cabin for passengers

hermit: a person who lives alone

palomino: a horse with a golden coat with a white and tail

regiment: a unit of ground forces

turret: a small tower

SAT GLOSSARY

coincidence: an occurrence of two or more events at one time by chance

eavesdropping: to secretly listen to a private conversation

mesmerized: to fascinate

perplexed: puzzled

recruit: a person signed up for service

Niagara Falls Trivia

1. Ten percent of the water of Niagara Falls flows over the American Falls. The other ninety percent flows over the Horseshoe Falls.

2. Today 50 percent of the Niagara River never makes it to the falls because it is diverted for power. This percentage increases to 75 percent at night and in the winter months.

3. The Niagara River is not a river; it is a strait.

4. One and a half million gallons of water flow through the Niagara River every second.

5. With power requirements and anti-erosion measures, erosion has been reduced to less than one foot a year.

6. Seven people have gone over the falls in a barrel. Only four survived!

7. A free swimmer has never conquered the lower rapids.

8. The famous Red Hill saved 28 people from death over the falls.

9. The first and only time both the American Falls and the Horseshoe Falls on the Canadian side fell silent was on the night of March 29, 1848. An ice jam formed on Lake Erie near Buffalo, blocking the water that flows along the Niagara River.

10. The word Niagara comes from the neutral Indian word *onguiaahra*, meaning "Thunder of Waters."

Scavenger Hunt

Want to have some fun? Let's go on a scavenger hunt! See if you can find the items below related to the mystery. (*Teachers: You have permission to reproduce this page for your students.*)

1. ___ A barrel

2. ___ A yellow raincoat

3. ___ Maid of the Mist

4. ___ Fort George

5. ___ The Loof Menagerie Carousel

6. ___ LEGO blocks

7. ___ An oxygen bar

8. ___ Canals and locks system

9. ___ Green water

10. ___ Gold

POP QUIZ

1. Who saved Grant's life at the beginning of the book?

2. What was the name of the boat that took the kids right next to Horseshoe Falls?

3. What was the name of the 63-year-old widow that went over the falls in a barrel?

4. Where did Christina find a clue in Brick City?

5. How many locks are between Lake Erie and Lake Ontario?

6. What is the legend of Goat's Island?

7. Who were the gold thieves?

8. Who was stuck inside a barrel at the winery?

Enjoy this exciting excerpt from:

THE COLONIAL CAPER MYSTERY AT

Williamsburg

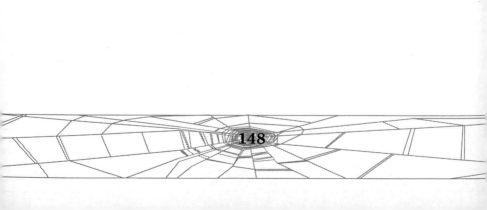

PROLOGUE

On a foggy autumn night, with golden-hued leaves pasted in a paisley pattern across a dirt road, a man wearing a wig white as snow, descended from a horse-drawn carriage.

He might have been George Washington... Thomas Jefferson...or Patrick Henry, but he wasn't. His name was never known. Indeed, save the evidence you are about to hear, there is no reason to believe that he ever passed through the ghostly, fogged-in village.

The village was, like all of America at that time, still ruled by England. As clouds scattered and the full moon peered out, the British Union Jack snapped sharp in the brisk breeze.

This village of Williamsburg, by daylight, the bustling, prosperous, and largest British colony in Virginia, now slept. No one ever saw the bewigged man stomp through the leaves to a large oak tree. As if by pre-plan and design, he tugged at a knothole and removed the wooden plug. Into the space, he placed an object and replaced the plug to stopper the hole tightly.

He returned to the carriage, to attend a ball? A funeral? An urgent mission of state? No one ever knew. The carriage sped off into the night. The tree grew taller over the years. The knothole kept the secret.

1

THE ROYAL COLONY

"We're doomed!" said Grant.

Christina, trying to finish her math homework in one of the back seats of the *Mystery Girl*, nodded in agreement. "You know Mimi won't let us take off without the pre-flight lecture, little brother. She always traps us like this! While Papa fuels the plane, we're her captives. Uh-oh, here she comes—get ready!"

Grant groaned and swiped his forehead. He sat in the pilot's seat while his grandfather held the fuel hose and grinned up at his grandson. Even he knew what their grandmother was about to do.

Sure enough, the airplane door flew open and Mimi, wearing her usual red suit and heels, popped into the other front seat of the airplane, tugging her ever-present tote bag of history research behind her.

As soon as she was settled, she blew kisses to her grandkids and began. "Now you know," she said, "we just can't leave Falcon Field here in Peachtree City and head for Virginia without me giving you some background, right?"

As she pulled a book out of her tote bag, she ignored Grant's groan but smiled when Christina slammed her math notebook closed and snapped to attention.

"Hurry, Papa, save us!" Grant squealed out the window.

"Now, Grant," said Mimi, "be still. You'll want to hear this! As you know, we're headed to Colonial Williamsburg in eastern Virginia. It was the former capital of the royal colony, before America was America."

"I thought Jamestown was the capital," said Christina.

"It was the first capital," Mimi explained. "But when the statehouse there burned, it was decided to move the capital to a new town. Williamsburg was named in honor of British King William III."

"And we care about all this—why?" groused Grant, leaning his head forward on the plane's steering wheel.

Mimi, who wrote mystery books filled with flabbergasting history for kids, looked appalled. "Why, because it's HISTORY! Our history. America's history!"

Grant still looked dissatisfied and thrust his head harder against the wheel. "But will there be a test?" he asked, unhappily.

Mimi sat back, relaxed, in her seat. She had a serious look on her usually smiling face. "Oh, Grant," she said, "when it comes to history, there's always a test. Many tests. And the outcome makes all the difference."

Christina knew her grandmother didn't mean a school test. She was just about to ask her what she did mean, when she felt a strange sensation. Suddenly, she reached across the front seat and grabbed her brother.

"Grant! Grant! Sit up!" she cried.

"THE PLANE IS MOVING!!"

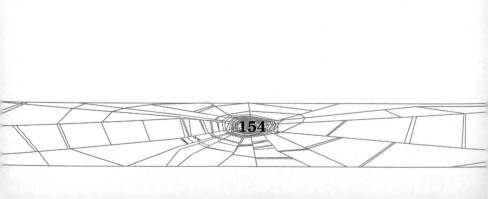

2

UNCLE WIG AND AUNT HALFPENNEY

"Stop! Stop!" shouted Christina and Mimi. Grant looked dumbfounded; what had he done, he wondered.

As his family went a little bonkers in the cockpit, Papa (called the Cowboy Pilot by Mimi), just whipped out the rope he always carried and lassoed the left strut of the barely moving airplane. "Got it!" he shouted up to them.

In a second, he had retrieved his rope, slapped his cowboy hat on his head, and hopped into the plane. Grant had already scurried to the back seat beside his sister, figuring he was in Big Trouble.

But his grandfather just grinned. "You gotta take flying lessons before you can fly, little buddy," he said with a wink.

Mimi fanned herself mightily with a travel brochure. "Oh my goodness! We're supposed to be going on an adventure, not having one right here on the tarmac even before we leave!"

Grant slunk lower in the backseat. To help her brother out and change the subject, Christina asked, "Can you tell us more about Colonial Williamsburg, please?" Grant gave his sister a "What are you thinking!" look.

Mimi sighed. "Oh, not right now," she said. "I'm too shook up. Maybe later, ok?"

In spite of themselves, Papa, Christina, and especially Grant, all laughed.

"Uh, ok, sure, Mimi," Grant finally said, trying to sound disappointed but failing miserably since he was spurting giggle spit at the same time. "We'll wait." And under his breath muttered, *Forever*.

Fortunately, the rest of the flight was uneventful. Everyone was **mesmerized** by the bright October sky, the counterpane quilt of colorful trees below, and the glint of ribbon rivers like silver thread in the sun. When the village of Colonial Williamsburg came into view, Christina gasped.

"Oh, Mimi!" she said. "It's beautiful—especially with the autumn colors. It looks just like a little pretend village."

Her grandmother nodded her blond curls toward the window. "Colonial Williamsburg is certainly one of the most beautiful historic sites in America. Tourists actually get to walk where history was constantly being made. America was just a baby back then!"

"History schmystery," grumbled Grant, waking up and stretching. "History's a mystery to me."

"No one said anything about mystery," Mimi insisted. "This is just a simple, quick, ordinary research trip. A quick tour. Some good colonial food. A little shopping..."

"Buying a million books..." Papa interrupted, banking the plane toward the final approach to the runway.

"Buying a million books..." Mimi agreed with a grin.

In the back, Christina and Grant cackled.

"What's so funny?" their grandmother demanded.

"You, Mimi!" said Christina. "You said no mystery. Where you go there's always a mystery!"

And sure enough, by the time they landed the plane, unloaded their luggage, caught a taxi into town, and got out in front of a colonial house, mystery was afoot!

"Welcome!" squealed Uncle Wig, adjusting his white powdered wig, which shifted nervously around his bald head.

"Get in here!" cried Aunt Halfpenny, shaking her white apron. "There's a mystery to solve and no time to lose!"